THE MAP
DROWNED
CITY

THE MAP OF THE DROWNED CITY

James Maxey

Cover art by James Maxey

First Printing

This is a standalone adventure excerpted from the novel **Dragonsgate: Spirits.**

The author may be contacted at
james@jamesmaxey.net

Newsletter signup at jamesmaxey.net

ISBN 9798529596050

We have lingered in the chambers of the sea
By sea-girls wreathed with seaweed red and brown

Till human voices wake us, and we drown.

T. S. Eliot

The Map of the Drowned City

Elspeth leaned from the riggings of the *Sea Dragon*, shielding her eyes from the glare of the bay, when she heard thumping from the forecastle. She leapt, plunging toward the sea as her father drunkenly called out, "Bring me my mermaid!"

Elspeth kept her body straight as a spear as she sliced into the water. She scissored her legs, swimming deeper. The sun cast her flickering shadow across the sandy avenues that covered the seafloor. On their spring visit to the Drowned City, the storm-swollen rivers that fed the bay had dumped so much silt that she'd barely been able to see her hand before her face. Now, as summer dried the inlands, the innumerable oysters of the bay filtered the waters to near transparency.

She glided over the bejeweled ridges that marked the ruined streets. Enormous crystalline shards, many as tall as houses, jutted at odd angles from rainbow sands of pulverized glass.

She came across the largest intact pane she'd ever seen, a rectangle of silver nearly as long as her ship. She swam closer, watching her reflection glide across the glass. The muted sun painted her skin with shimmering scales of blue and green. Her long hair floated around her in a halo as she drifted.

For a moment, she fantasized that she truly was a mermaid, stolen from her kingdom and forced to live among ship-bound brutes. Any moment a fish-king with a crown and trident might swim forth to guide her to her castle of coral.

She cherished these quiet moments, far from groaning ropes and thumping sails, safe from surly voices and slurred curses. The distant murmur of surf rolled along her skin, not so different from the heartbeat a baby must hear in the womb.

Of course, at eleven years of age, Elspeth was no baby, and she was no mermaid. She was the daughter of Portsmouth Howell, no matter how much she wished it were not so. But wishes would never bring order, safety, or comfort to her world. Hard and cynical before her time, her father had taught her well that all desirable things in life could only be purchased with gold. Turning her face toward the sun, she kicked, rising toward the great, grim shadow of her father's ship.

Elspeth drew breath as she breached the surface. As water drained from her ears the chaos of the *Sea Dragon* wafted over the waters. Her father still shouted for her, and his rising anger had crewmen racing about the deck, attempting to look busy while avoiding actual labor.

The only motionless figure was Surgeon. The dragon was perched in the rigging, his long, scaly face turned toward her. Surgeon was a tatterwing, a sky-dragon whose wings had been cut to ribbons in punishment for some crime. No one aboard ship knew or cared what might have earned him such a fate. Nor did anyone care what his true name might have been. The crew called him Surgeon because the beast was, in fact, a competent surgeon. He had an encyclopedic knowledge of human anatomy, and his pills, potions, and poultices cured more maladies than they caused. Despite this, every sailor aboard cursed the filthy beast, though never to his face. Surgeon's claws could slice a man open as skillfully as they could sew a wound shut.

"Where's my mermaid!" her father screamed, his voice echoing in the hold, followed by a loud crash.

Surgeon tossed down a rope. "You should go to your father before he tears the ship apart."

"Do you know what he wants with me?" she asked.

"What does he ever want you for, other than to dive for treasure?"

For most people adrift at sea, the rope dangling before her would have been a lifeline. She stared at it like a condemned man looking upon a noose.

Surgeon noted her hesitation. "We're only a few miles from shore. I never saw you if you choose to swim away forever."

Elspeth sighed. "Who then would care for my mother?"

She grasped the rope and started to climb.

"Someone bring her to me!" her father shrieked as he came up the ladder from the hold at the same time she swung herself over the railing. Her father had a bottle in his good hand as he waved the hook that capped his other arm. "I want my mermaid!"

None of the men on deck bothered to look in his direction. Portsmouth Howell's captain's coat was unbuttoned, revealing his shirtless torso, pockmarked with festering boils. His long, dark hair hung in tangles around his face. His tricorn hat had blown overboard weeks ago, meaning he had nothing to shield his eyes as he looked into the rigging still seeking Elspeth, staring right into the sun. He winced, closing his eyes as he shook his bottle of liquor at the sky, growling, "Son of the Devil!"

As he gesticulated toward the sun, his pants slipped from his boney hips, catching at his knees. He bent to retrieve them, toppling face first to the deck.

"Assassin!" her father shouted, rolling to his back, slashing the air with his hook. "I'll flay the villain that tripped me!"

"No one tripped you, father," said Elspeth, stepping toward him. She crouched, helping him pull his pants up, then steadying him as he rose. Never once did he let go of his bottle.

"Where've you been?" he asked, sounding more confused than angry.

"Swimming," she said, as if the water streaming from her hair, blouse, and britches failed to make that obvious. "While you slept, we reached the Drowned City." She started to add, "No thanks to you," but held her tongue.

Though she was only eleven, Elspeth had made this journey countless times. Her father's men were the worst Hampton had to offer, louts too stupid, lazy, or degraded to find work on respectable vessels. On any other ship, a captain as abusive as Portsmouth Howell would have been the target of mutiny, but her father had assembled a crew too slovenly and stupid to unite against him.

None of these men could use a sextant or read a map. Elspeth had navigated the *Sea Dragon* along the parlous coast, through the gauntlet of pirates and shoals that lay between Hampton and the Drowned City. While she lacked her father's ability to tongue-lash his disheveled crew into chaotic action, the less dimwitted seamen grasped that Elspeth knew what she was doing. They followed her commands because she was their best hope of returning from a voyage alive.

Elspeth tried to navigate her father back to his cabin but he couldn't keep his legs under him. A shadow fell across them both and she turned to find Surgeon. Wordlessly, the dragon grabbed her father, rudely slinging him across his back like a filthy duffle bag. Surgeon carried him to his cabin and tossed him on the bunk. The dragon doused the captain with the contents of a bucket next to the bed. Elspeth held her breath, sparing her lungs from the reeking fumes.

Her father sat up, sputtering, wiping his face, his eyes wide.

"You've found your mermaid," Surgeon said. "Show her the map."

Portsmouth glowered at Surgeon. "How do you know about the map?"

"You were boasting about it before we ever left port."

"I was?" asked her father. He nodded slowly. "Aye. Tis a thing of beauty! I'm going to be richer than Albekizan!" His brow furrowed. "You'll get your taste, you greedy dog. Now be gone! The map's not for your devil eyes."

"As you wish," said Surgeon, turning away. The dragon's gaze lingered on Elspeth for a long second. He seemed on the verge of speaking, before changing his mind and leaving.

Elspeth was glad he hadn't asked her a question since she was still holding her breath. Her mother's family, the Bloodsworths, came from the Blades, a chain of long, thin islands far beyond the eastern horizon. Women of these isles fed their families by spearfishing among the reefs of the archipelago. Elspeth had inherited her mother's powerful lungs.

Beneath the waves, she could swim for nearly ten minutes before resurfacing. With luck, her father would tell her what he had planned before she had to take another breath in the rancid atmosphere of his cabin.

Her father rolled from his bunk, landing in a crouch, then stood and lurched for his desk. He dramatically swept aside the clutter of empty bottles and scrawled ledgers, then fumbled beneath the desk with his hook, muttering curses.

Elspeth gently nudged him aside, reached beneath the desk, and pressed the latch that popped open the hidden drawer. Her father pulled out a scroll of yellowed paper and unrolled it. "Behold!" he said. "The key to my fortune!"

Her heart sank. She'd seen this map before, or ones like it. In the narrow alleys of Hampton, dealers sold antiquities from the antediluvian world. Long ago, the coasts were cluttered with great metropolises teeming with wonders, including towers of glass that pierced the heavens. Mankind had grown so powerful that they no longer feared the gods. In retribution, the gods caused the sea to rise, destroying the cities.

Elspeth doubted the existence of gods. The sea, the wind, and the sun needed no guiding intelligence to destroy the works of man. Still, the magnificent cities of lore were no myth. When she ran her fingers through the sands of any beach, she pulled up fragments of this lost age, worn bricks and rusted blobs, the occasional coin, and innumerable sand-frosted pebbles of glass. In shallow bays, parallel rows of oyster beds marked out ancient avenues of towns long forgotten. The Drowned City was the largest of these vanished places. When the water was calm and clear, anyone could see the grid of streets covering endless miles of seafloor.

"This street," her father said, tapping the map. "This street was where the banks were."

She didn't understand why that mattered at all. Her father's unsteady finger was pointing to a street that was plainly inland. The bank where the land bordered the bay was several blocks distant from his finger.

Portsmouth recognized doubt in her face. "I'm not speaking of a shoreline. I'm talking about the type of bank where treasures are held. The vaults of these banks were filled with gold and silver and precious gems. Find them, and my fortune is made!"

She rolled her eyes, having heard all this before.

"It's different this time!" he said. "There are tons of gold in these vaults! Literal tons!"

The absurdity of his words defeated her resolve not to breathe inside his cabin. She said, "If it's a literal ton, how am I supposed to swim back up with it?"

"Find it and I'll figure it out."

"Have you figured out how I'm supposed to get into a vault?"

"Iron doors will have corroded away," said her father. "The gold will just be lying there, pristine and for the taking!"

"Nothing down there is pristine," she said. "These banks you're looking for collapsed long ago."

"The vaults would be in basements, untouched by the waves."

"If there are any basements, they're filled with silt."

"Not all of them," said her father. "Mary told me of the tunnels she found. She said there's a city beneath the city. This map tells me where to find the entrances to these tunnels."

"I know about the tunnels," Elspeth admitted. "The ones I've found are pitch black. You want me to grope around in the dark? That's your big plan?"

"I've figured that out!" said her father, staggering toward his bunk. He dropped to his knees, thrusting his good arm far beneath his bed. He pulled out a small wooden crate barely big enough to hold a loaf of bread. "Feast your eyes on these," he said, prying the lid open with his hook. He revealed a row of red cylinders, each about a foot long and maybe an inch and a half thick. "Flares! Do you know how rare these are?"

"Oh my stars," said Elspeth, who did know how rare they were. Thanks to her father's lust for lost treasures, she knew more than most people about the relics of the antediluvian world. These red cylinders had once been relatively common objects. A flare was full of a substance that burned brightly, even underwater. The passage of centuries had turned these once mundane items into precious rarities. Her father's mad plan was to search for phantom gold using antiquities worth more than their weight in gold.

"How did you get these?" she asked.

"Never mind that," he said.

"You want me to burn through a fortune in rare artifacts for the chance of finding a few gold coins?"

"It's not a few coins we're seeking," he said. "You'll find bricks of gold. Bricks! And diamonds big as apples!"

"But these flares could pay our debts. The *Sea Dragon* could sail into Hampton without being seized by our creditors. You could get our house back, and–"

"You dream small, daughter," said Portsmouth. "The devil take my creditors!" He drew up to his full height, straightening his captain's coat, and hitching up his sagging britches. He puffed out his chest as he said, "Those coin-sharks spend their days fiddling over numbers on a ledger, blind to the true riches of this world. When we sail back to Hampton with a ship laden with treasure, they'll erect statues to the force of nature that is Portsmouth Howell!"

Of course, there was already a statue of a Howell standing in Hampton. Elspeth's grandfather was Samson Howell, the legendary commander of the Salt Fleet. Before meeting his untimely death in a storm, Samson had given his young son Portsmouth command of his finest ship, the *Sea Dragon*. Inheriting a well-established trade route and the good name of his father, Portsmouth Howell had been handed a foolproof path toward his own fortune. But, the first time Portsmouth had navigated the *Sea Dragon* from its home port, he set a course not for Sharlston, the contracted destination of his cargo, but for the distant Blades. The beautiful Mary Bloodsworth had rebuffed his drunken proposal two years before, when he was but a lad of seventeen. Returning as the captain of his own ship, Mary saw the young sailor with different eyes, and said yes.

Portsmouth celebrated their nuptials with a voyage to the Drowned City. His cargo was already weeks late. What would another month matter?

The sandbars surrounding the city were treacherous to navigate, but the glittering, glassy ruins were a wonderful gift to a diver like Mary.

Mary discovered statues of long forgotten men, their names and faces blotted out by barnacles. She swam through great, roofless halls, sifting through the bejeweled sand for simple treasures. She found an old tea cup with a gilded rim, a porcelain doll with a painted red dress, and fragile glass tubes bent and twisted to form letters. On the last night of their stay, on a moonlit dive, Mary had dragged her fingers through fine sand and came up holding a glittering gold necklace studded with diamonds.

When Mary had handed Portsmouth the necklace, she handed over a fortune worth more than all the cargo in the hold of the *Sea Dragon*. She didn't know she was also handing over all her hopes and her happiness, to be crushed in his greedy fingers.

Portsmouth Howell climbed the riggings with his spyglass tucked beneath his chin. Elspeth had no doubt her father would find this street of banks among the avenues of shells. For longer than she'd been alive, her father had obsessively studied the city. Her two older sisters, long since lost to the sea, had dragged up old street signs, which her father had cross-referenced with his collection of ancient maps. Her family had never found another treasure quite as valuable as the necklace, but they'd pulled up smaller trinkets, wedding bands, earrings and gold nuggets shaped like human teeth. Bowls and plates and glassware emerged from the sand looking new. The antiquities fetched good prices, but never quite paid the expenses of the trips. The worse their finances grew, the more frequently Portsmouth returned to the Drowned City in pursuit of his great fortune.

The loss of two daughters hadn't dissuaded him. Their bodies had never been found. As Elspeth went below deck to the small cabin near the rear of the ship, she found herself thinking of these lost sisters, whether she might one day find their bones among the ruins, or whether they'd taken their chances by swimming for the untamed shores surrounding the bay.

She knocked once on the door of the small cabin. There was no answer. She went inside. A single open window ventilated the small space, with a ragged curtain fluttering before it. Her mother was tucked beneath covers, her hand draped across her eyes. Elspeth could tell that she was awake.

"We've reached the Drowned City?" Mary asked.

"Aye," said Elspeth.

"Your father won't be satisfied until all our bones roll beneath the waves," said Mary.

"This might be the last time we make this journey," said Elspeth. "Father has a map that leads to vaults of gold."

"Then our doom is certain," said Mary, still covering her eyes.

"It might be different this time," said Elspeth. "Imagine if we were rich. We could have a house in Hampton again. We could live comfortably, among respectable people."

"Your father owned a house when I married him," said her mother. "The name Howell was respectable, once." Her mother lifted her head, rising on her elbows. "Help me with the bed pan."

Elspeth moved to her mother's side. She'd been Mary's primary caretaker for the last four years, ever since her mother had lost the use of her legs.

Mary said, "Don't be seduced by your father's dreams of treasure."

"But we've found treasure before," said Elspeth. "And I'm not doing this for his dream. I'm doing it for mine. I want to take you from the chaos of this ship. I want you to be safe and comfortable. The gold that will save us is down there, I know it. I just need a little luck."

"My luck finding that necklace ruined us all."

"You can't blame yourself," said Elspeth.

"I can and I shall," Mary said bitterly. "I'm the one who awakened the monster. One day, it shall devour us."

Elspeth wasn't certain if her mother spoke metaphorically of her father, or referred to the actual sea monster that she claimed dwelled in the subterranean chambers of the city.

"Whatever your father wants, don't swim into the tunnels," Mary warned, which resolved the ambiguity. She was speaking of the actual beast. For the hundredth time, Mary gave her warning of the monster haunting the drowned city: "The beast that crushed my legs has tentacles thicker than the trunk of an ancient oak. No matter how much your father tempts you with tales of treasure, never swim into the undercity. If I lose you, I'll have nothing."

"You'll always have me," said Elspeth, as she emptied the bedpan out the window. "I swear this is our last trip to these terrible waters. I'm going to buy us a house, and hire a nurse, and give you the life of a queen."

Mary's eyes glistened. "It pains me that I chain you down."

"Caring for you is no burden."

Her mother shook her head. "The only reason your father keeps me aboard instead of dumping me at some house of charity is that I shackle you to him.

As long as I live, you can't escape."

"I swear, after this trip, all will be different," said Elspeth.

Mary wept uncontrollably at these reassuring words. No doubt her mother had heard them before, from her father's lips.

Elspeth left her mother's tiny cabin, returning to the hold. The exposed ribs of the ship curved around her in the large, dimly lit space, making her feel like she was in the belly of some enormous beast. In the shadows of the far wall, two golden eyes watched her.

It was Surgeon. She shuddered at the sight of him. In the air, sky-dragons seemed huge, with twenty-foot wingspans and powerful chests and shoulders. Stripped of their wings, they weren't terribly fearsome. Surgeon was only a little taller than she was, and his wingless forelimbs were thin, almost skeletal, though inhumanly strong. The dragon's claws would be the envy of any panther, but it wasn't his claws that gave him such a sinister air.

There was something about his gaze that made her feel like a mouse staring into the eyes of a cat.

Surgeon said, with a disinterested tone, "Your only escape will be to kill him."

"What?" she asked.

"You could follow the example of the dragon kings," said Surgeon. "They drive away their sons when they reach the age of maturity. The spurned sons either perish in the wilderness, or grow stronger in their exile until they return to slay their father. In this way, the kingdom is always ruled by a dragon of great strength."

"Why are you telling me this?"

"I've lived among humans for a long time," said Surgeon. "I've never before known a child who commanded her own ship."

"This is my father's ship," Elspeth said, clenching her fists. "If you continue to speak with such insolence, I'll have you keelhauled for mutiny."

"Yes," said Surgeon. "You'd take charge of the task yourself. The last three times we've put to sea, your father has barely given an order. The crew waits for your commands."

"They know I speak for my father."

"They know your father babbles and blusters, while you give sensible orders that will return them safely back to port."

"My father has many things on his mind," she said, crossing her arms. "I'm merely helping."

"Such loyalty. You'll never keep the promises you make to your mother while your father still breathes."

"You were eavesdropping?"

"Dragons hear everything," said Surgeon. "Men fear my claws, but it's my ears that have kept me alive all these years."

"Those years will come to a swift end if you continue to speak of mutiny."

"Then let us speak of treasure."

Her curiosity was stirred. The dragon was too intelligent to reveal himself as a mutineer unless the payoff was genuine. "What treasure do you speak of?"

"Look around," said Surgeon. "What do you see?"

She shrugged. "The hold?"

"The *empty* hold," said Surgeon. "The ribs of this vessel should be groaning with the weight of cargo. Your father inherited all he needed to build his fortune. This ship is all that remains, but it's no small prize."

"I don't need you to tell me my family history," she said.

"Then let me tell you your future. Despite all your father has done to besmirch his name, if you take command of this vessel, your Howell ancestry will open many doors."

"You truly believe anyone would entrust their cargo to a ship captained by a girl my age?"

"The audacity of the proposition is what makes it attractive," said Surgeon. "Investors are gamblers at heart. But this need not be a gamble on *your* part. I've the wealth you'd need to pay your debts."

"You? Wealthy?" She'd overestimated the dragon's grasp of reality.

"I haven't always been a tatterwing," Surgeon said, raising his bony forelimbs, shaking the remnant shreds of his wings. "I held a high office at the College of Spires. I studied artifacts and manuscripts from the antediluvian world, a time before dragons even existed."

"Haven't dragons been around forever?" she asked, as her doubts grew about his sanity.

"Dragons didn't appear until roughly a thousand years ago. As a scholar of the Human Age, the origin of dragons seems plain enough. Humans mastered the codes that organize non-living molecules into the various forms of life. The obvious conclusion is that humans created dragons."

"Really?" said Elspeth. She had no idea what a molecule was, living or non-living. The only reason she couldn't comfortably dismiss his talk as gibberish was that in all her journeys through the Drowned City, she'd never once found any sign of dragons. Every artifact she'd ever dug up had plainly been crafted for use by humans.

"It was a great honor to be able to study the Human Age. The High Biologian took care in selecting dragons who could be trusted with this scholarship. For many years, I did nothing to betray this trust." He shook his head slowly. "But dragons aren't the only ones who study antiquities. There are isolated communities of humans who cling to the old knowledge. I was eager to learn what they knew. Doing so required clandestine trades of my documents for theirs. My superiors learned of my collaboration with humans... and..." The rest of his story trailed off as he scratched at the ragged scars that marred his limbs. "Your father routinely tosses aside trash brought up in his obsessive search for gold. Within these cast-off clumps of shell and mud, I find remnants of lost technologies."

"I've found old gears and cables," said Elspeth. "But it's all ruined. Useless."

"Who cares about gears and cables?" asked Surgeon. "The greatest machines of men moved information, not cargo. Vast libraries of knowledge could be inscribed on a tiny wafer of silicon. The infusion of so much information into such a compact space brought forth a new form of life, machines that could think."

Elspeth let out a deep sigh. That settled things. The dragon was insane.

Surgeon didn't notice her skepticism. He continued: "These silicon chips were ubiquitous, embedded in everyday objects. The devices that contain the chips seldom endure beneath the sea, but often the chips themselves were sealed for protection against the elements. My human contacts pay handsomely for these chips. I've accumulated a respectable fortune."

"Yet you still work as a sailor," she said.

"A tatterwing with wealth would draw unwelcome attention. I use human agents to manage my affairs. Your father fears his creditors will seize the *Sea Dragon*, never suspecting that I'm his primary investor. His journeys to the Drowned City have been very helpful to me."

"If you're benefiting from my father's actions, why speak of mutiny?"

"Your father wearies me. He's too unreliable and too greedy to be trusted. If you were in command, our partnership would prove most fruitful."

"I would hardly be trustworthy if I betrayed my father," she said.

"You're only betraying yourself if you continue to serve him. You want order, safety, and comfort for your mother. Your father stands between you and your needs. I can help you. In return, you can help me obtain the one thing I truly desire."

"Which is?"

"Revenge!" said Surgeon, his eyes flashing as he gazed upon his ruined wings. "My fellow dragons thought I was dangerous. I intend to prove them right!"

"You're as mad as my father," said Elspeth.

Before Surgeon could say anything to dispute this, her father's voice rang out from above, calling for his mermaid. She turned from Surgeon, fully intending to recount this conversation to her father. Yet, before she reached the deck, she decided to say nothing for the moment. Order, safety, and comfort. Could Surgeon's tiny treasures truly purchase these things?

It was late afternoon. The air was thick and menacing, ripe for a storm though there wasn't a cloud in the sky.

"By the stars, I've found it!" her father said from high in the crow's nest, bidding her to climb the riggings to join him.

From the heights, she studied the waters. The grid of long, straight avenues of the ancient city could be seen in rows of light and shadow.

"Remember the stone towers we found?" her father asked.

She nodded, remembering the bulky structures, evenly spaced in a straight line that ran nearly a mile.

"Bridge posts," Portsmouth said, tapping a line on the map that crossed a finger of blue. "And if the bridge was there, the waterfront was yonder."

She nodded again as he pointed. She'd swam in that area before, finding an old seawall, with ruins on one side and deep water beyond, and concrete pilings that might have once supported docks.

"And if that's the waterfront, then we're over the street of banks!" He drew a long, loud sniff. "The treasure is so close I can smell it!"

"If you say so," she mumbled.

"That's my girl!" she said, wrapping his hook arm around her shoulders in an awkward hug.

They climbed back down to the deck so that her father could get the flares. Her father went into his cabin while she waited on the deck. When her father stepped back through the doorway, Surgeon hopped down from the riggings, landing face to face with the man.

"Demon!" her father growled, reaching toward his scabbard. His fingers closed around empty air where a hilt should have been. Drawing back his shoulders, Portsmouth said, "You're lucky I didn't run you through. Have a care!"

"Care is in short supply these days," said Surgeon. "Don't you know where we are?"

"Of course," said Portsmouth. "I brought us here, did I not?"

"I don't doubt your navigation, only your memory," said Surgeon, pointing toward the distant shoreline. "We can't be more than a hundred yards from the area where your mate was attacked. Let's find safer waters to explore."

"You ungrateful turd!" Portsmouth's spittle sprayed across the dragon's face. "You were a starving beggar when you came crawling to me! I didn't bring you aboard to question my orders! Get out of my sight or I'll use your sorry hide for a new pair of boots!" Her father raised his hook, looking as if he intended to slash the dragon. Surgeon didn't retreat.

Her father lowered his arm, "To hell with you! Keep your damned snout out of my business."

Surgeon looked at Elspeth.

She said, "I'll dive where my captain tells me to dive."

Surgeon nodded, then stepped aside.

Elspeth looked toward the distant shore. She'd been so young when her mother had been hurt. Was this the place? The land looked identical to hundreds of other miles of feral coastline. Her jaw tightened as the memories of her mother's screams came back to her.

Then she was in the water, swimming along avenues of glass, alone in the magnificent desolation, a mermaid princess surveying her kingdom of shells. It was an empty kingdom, but still more of a home than the ship, where she was orphaned by her father's madness and her mother's grief. The temptation to never again rise toward the air crept into her mind, lingering only a moment, before she chased it out like an unwelcome guest.

Clutching the rake she carried more firmly, she weighed the words of her mother and father. Her mother wanted her to stay out of the tunnels. Her father wanted her to search for treasure in the undercity.

Her father's plan, despite the risks, held the most appeal. Order, safety, and comfort – Surgeon had diagnosed her needs well. Her father's bottomless greed could never be satisfied, but gold, properly spent, could purchase the better life she craved.

She stood in the center of the avenue. Her weighted belt and heavy rake pressed her outstretched toes into the glassy sand. In pale ghost light beneath shimmering waves she could imagine the city at twilight, with candles and lanterns flickering in windows. Anemones bloomed where flowerbeds once stood, as lazy nurse sharks swam in and out of doorways where merchants and maidens once strolled.

She wondered if the deluge had come as a single wave, or inch by inch, over decades. The people who lived here might have watched the waters claim one cobblestone at a time, year after year, until endless loss became the normal course of life, and none could remember that the streets had once been dry.

Walking slowly, raking at lumps, she turned up fragments of old junk. An intact saucer caught her eye and she stuffed it into the sack slung over her shoulder. She continued her journey, making discoveries with each sweep of the rake, dismissing all she found as worthless. Bottles, buttons, encrusted bolts and nails. Her tines caught an odd bit of yellow rope that couldn't be pulled free, so she moved on. She found a battered orange cone trapped beneath a flat rock that cracked apart when she lifted it. The cone was made of stiff rubber, with a large open top surrounded by a flat square lip and a hole at the narrow end big enough to stick two fingers in. What the container might have held eluded her. She tossed it aside.

She kicked back to the surface for another breath. Her father called her name, and shouted out the direction he wanted her to swim. She dove without acknowledging him. She sank next to a relatively straight and flat wall. In a few stray spots not covered by shellfish, loops of green paint fluoresced in fingered rays of sunlight. Gliding around the broken wall, she found a deep pit with a series of shallow ledges descending through the sand. It was an old staircase, leading underground. She drifted downward until she reached the ghost of a door, a paper-thin barrier of lacy lime and fragmented rust. Beyond was darkness, black and formless.

She pushed her rake through the remnant door, tearing it to pieces. She probed the darkness, sweeping side to side, up, down, until the tines hit the floor. She drug the rake across a surface that felt like tile. She waved away the swirling sediment dragged out by the tines. Something yellow flashed among fragments of shell. She snatched it up, unable to believe her eyes. Gold! A whole rod of it, thinner than her little finger, but nearly as long as her hand. Only, it didn't weigh as much as it should. It was a hollow tube, not a solid rod. Similar tubes littered the seabed, though this was the first she'd found made of gold. Sometimes there were words on the shaft, like "Bic" and "Sharpie." This one bore the words "Elijah Industries." It must have been sheltered in darkness ever since the city flooded. Gold didn't corrode in seawater, but even faint sunlight would hide gold beneath a crust of lime.

She raked into the room once more, straining to fully extend her arm. She felt the tip push against a few bits of rubble, some heavy, some she could move around. She dragged out a fist-sized lump. It proved to be a figurine, an orange cat, sitting with its hind legs splayed out before it, holding a big cup against its belly. Some of the glaze had flaked off the ears, revealing white ceramic beneath. The ceramic would have turned green if light ever penetrated the room.

She decided the room beyond was worth a closer look. She had two flares tucked into her pants, though they would have to wait. Her lungs were full of needle pricks. Turning her face upward, she scissored her legs and rose.

When she reached the surface, gulls were all around. Over their cries, her father called out, "Have you found my gold, mermaid?"

She swam toward the ship, holding up the ceramic cat. Her father lowered a basket for her to put it in. She could see the disappointment in his eyes. She kept the golden tube, to add to her private stash of easily hidden loot that might one day purchase order, safety, and comfort.

High overhead, in the crow's nest, Surgeon's inhuman form was a silhouette against a white sky.

Elspeth dove. It took less than a minute to return to the stairs. With a final kick, she glided into the darkness beyond, a flare held tightly in her hand. With clenched teeth, she pulled the cap free.

Instantly, she was blind. She turned her face away, her eyes clamped shut. Bright red filled the interior of her eyelids. Her hand started to burn as the flare boiled the water near the tip, forcing her to drop the light.

She kept her eyes closed until the glow faded, wasting a precious minute of air. When her vision returned, the light surrounding her was hellish red, with her shadow a looming devil cast upward by the flare. Despite the odd lighting, she could make out the contours of the room well enough. To her great surprise, there was a wooden desk near the far wall, and beyond it was an open doorway. She'd never seen anything made of wood survive in such perfect condition before. She kicked, drifting toward it, until she hovered over it. On the far side, she saw drawers, including a long center one slightly ajar. She reached out to open it further.

The second her fingers touched the wooden handle, the whole desk collapsed into a cloud of loose, brown, gelatinous fragments that looked like diarrhea. As the cloud calmed, glints caught her eye.

Coins! They were tightly sealed in a transparent bag. She picked up the bag, which felt, vaguely, like a sausage casing, thin and tough. There were several dozen coins within the bag, of four different sizes. Three of the sizes were made of a dull silver, but the most common coins within the bag were brown. All were stamped with the heads of men, proof of their antiquity. Modern coins bore the visages of dragons.

Further sifting through the brown muck produced a picture frame, with a ghostly family imprinted on the glass. She found a small, round mirror, cracked in half, and more of the hollow tubes, though none were made of gold.

She turned her attention to the doorway. If there had been a door once, it had long since rotted. She poked her head inside. Unfortunately, the flare behind her failed to cast much light into the room. She could barely make out a boxy shape about two yards inside the room. She threw the tines of her rake across it and dragged it closer. It turned out to be a large flattened rectangle made of a tough, shell-like material. Despite being large enough for her to curl up inside it, the object weighed practically nothing. The sealed case obviously had air trapped within, leaving it neutrally buoyant. The face of the case had raised letters that matched those on the golden tube she'd found: Elijah Industries.

She ran the strap of her canvas bag through a handle along the edge of the case then slung it over her back. Her lungs tingled. She needed to return to the surface. Curiosity overpowered caution, and she leaned far into the darkness, her rake outstretched as far as it could go.

Instead of striking a second case, her rake fell upon something firm but yielding, as if she was pushing the tines into a featherbed. No, it was more like the time they'd found the freshly beached whale, the way the skin had felt when poked with driftwood.

Without warning, a swirl of water tossed her backward. The rake tore from her hand. Her head banged against the upper frame of the door as the violent current carried her back into the first room, where the flare danced and skittered across the floor, casting turbulent shadows. Her eyes fixed on the door she'd just been forced out of. Something was moving across it, like a dark, mottled gray curtain, fluttering and flapping. The rolling gray halted, leaving a single shape centered in the doorframe. An eye! The size of a wagon wheel, with a copper and teal iris surrounding a pupil dark as the abyss.

Terror seized her. She kicked and twisted, her arms windmilling, her whole body writhing in uncontrolled panic. Her disjointed motions brought her no closer to the stairs that led to escape. She'd turned in a full circle, and was now facing the interior door again. The eye was gone, as was the gray curtain. Had it only been her imagination? A hallucination brought about by lack of air?

Then a tentacle groped from the doorway, thicker than a yardarm, covered in large, grasping suckers. It probed blindly toward her, until the tip brushed against the burning flare.

Instantly, the tentacle drew back.

She fought to control her fear. It was only an octopus! True, it was the largest she'd ever seen, but that was in her favor, wasn't it? Nothing that big could possibly fit through the door.

As soon as she had the thought, the octopus proved her wrong, as its boneless body started flowing through the gap. She decided not to wait to see if all of it could really make it through. She whirled, swimming for the stairs.

All at once, everything went black. Had the flare burned out? She reached back and grabbed the second flare. She held it tightly as she pulled the cap free. Nothing! No light at all.

Before she tossed the useless flare away, some voice in the back of her mind screamed not to do so. The door to the staircase should have been a rectangle of light no matter what the flare was doing. The water around her hand was growing hot. She couldn't see the door or the flare because the octopus had filled the water with ink.

Fortunately, as the huge beast flowed into the room, water flowed out, tumbling her through the door and up the stairs, the water growing grayer, until at last she could see the dark hull of the *Sea*

Dragon. She unfastened her weighted belt. She tried to slip off her bag, ridding herself of the bulky case, but with all her panicked twisting she'd tangled the strap and had no time to waste trying to get free. Straining every muscle, she swam for the surface still holding onto the flare. The octopus had recoiled from its heat. As long as she kept moving, the hot water flowing across her hand was bearable.

Just as she was most hungry for a lifesaving breath, something wrapped around her leg. With the surface mere inches away, she was jerked down. Her leg felt like it was being torn from her hip. She cried out in agony. Life sustaining air undulated toward the surface in silvery bubbles. Beneath her, the octopus expanded across the sea floor. The beast looked large enough to swallow a whale. The tentacle grasping her leg had to be at least fifty feet long. To her relief, her leg was still connected to her body.

Despite the surprise attack, she'd kept her desperate grasp on the flare. She jammed the blazing tip against the tentacle that trapped her. The tentacle released her, its raspy suckers tearing moon-shaped chunks of flesh from her leg as it recoiled. Despite the pain, she swam for the surface, trying to ignore the gushing clouds of pink pulsing from her leg.

With a final push, her head popped above the surface. She gulped precious air. The fresh breath left her giddy. She'd survive this yet! She spun in the water, searching for the *Sea Dragon*. The ship bobbed in the breeze, its sails unfurling. She heard her father screaming, "Faster, you scurvy dogs, faster!"

She furrowed her brow. She appreciated her father's sense of urgency in wanting to save her, but the ship was fifty feet away. They didn't need to raise the sails, they only needed to toss her a rope.

Her eyes found her father, leaning out over the side of the ship. He wasn't looking at her. He was looking into the depths. He cried out, "Tis the kraken! He'll swallow us all if you laggards don't snap to!"

Her father hadn't raised the sails to rescue her. He was saving himself! Did he think the creature had already swallowed her? Did he care if she was alive or not?

She tried to swim but her leg, bloodied and half-wrenched from its socket, wouldn't cooperate. She stopped flailing as a triangular fin cut an arc through the water not more than twenty yards off. It was a bull shark, and a big one. She swam among sharks all the time, but never while bleeding. She called out to the ship, but there was no sign anyone heard her.

She hung in the water, motionless and silent. She let the flare drop from her fingers. Between the octopus and the shark and the bulky case threatening to pull her under, all her fears collided, then collapsed, producing a curious calm.

As clarity settled over her mind, she thought of the people of the Drowned City, of whether the waters killed them swift or slow, and whether that mattered at all. The world offered no safety and no comfort. But order? Order had ruled her all along. Her life followed the same grand plan all humanity must follow. She'd been born, she would die, and all that happened in between meant nothing at all to the sun, the wind, and the sea.

Then a lifebuoy splashed into the water only a few feet away.

Surgeon stood at the rail near the rudder, clasping the buoy rope.

"Grab hold!"

She splashed her way toward the buoy, flopping like a wounded seal. She reached the rope and twisted it around her forearm. Surgeon braced himself against the rail, straining as he pulled the rope.

"Blast you!" her father screamed as he ran up to Surgeon. "I sent you to the wheel! Move or I'll flay your accursed hide!"

Surgeon ignored the captain. Portsmouth grabbed a belaying pin and brandished it menacingly. Surgeon kept to his task, dragging Elspeth through the water with all the speed his inhuman muscles could summon. In seconds, Elspeth was close enough to the hull to touch it. When Surgeon tried to pull her from the water, the instant the case strapped to her back cleared the waves it lost its buoyancy and turned into an anchor. The rope slipped from Surgeon's grasp and she splashed back into the drink.

Before Surgeon could attempt to haul her up again, the unfurled mainsail caught wind at a bad angle. The ship rolled toward her. The looming bulk smashed into her, the barnacles of the hull hooking into her face and shoulders like the claws of a thousand cats, dragging her beneath the surface. The rope still wrapped around her arm had fallen slack, but jerked taut as the ship rolled in the other direction, lifting her from the water. She lost her grip on the rope and tore her hands attempting to halt her slide across the barnacles into the churning water. One second she was in the air, the next her world turned into bloody foam and rainbow bubbles, dazzling light and indecipherable darkness. Sweeping her arms, she managed to push away from the ship, getting distance from the barnacles, but still tossed by swells that lifted her and plunged her down.

Righting herself in the water, she craned her neck to see if the shark was any nearer. It was. The predator was no more than ten feet away, shooting straight toward her. The gray fin rose nearly a yard above the water, a true behemoth of a shark.

The sea mounded. A gaping, toothy cavern opened, sucking her toward her death. Then, the shark came to a sudden halt. It whipped into the air, revealing a body at least thirty feet long. Wrapped around this body was a massive tentacle. The shark wriggled as a mountainous form rose beneath it. With a jerk, the shark vanished beneath the surface. The swirling water pulled Elspeth under. Through the churn she saw the shark shoved beneath the mantle of the octopus. Her eardrums rang as the creature's beak snapped shut on its struggling prey.

As the octopus gulped down its meal, the creature fixed its wagon wheel eyes upon Elspeth. She stared into the twin voids of its pupils, looking for mercy, finding only hunger.

Before the tentacles could grasp her, something sharp and strong clamped onto her shoulder. She was yanked from the water, then clasped roughly against Surgeon's boney ribs. The dragon dangled from the buoy rope, which had been swiftly lashed to the rail.

"You weigh... more... than I expected," Surgeon said through gritted teeth. "What's in that chest?"

"I hope we find out!" she said.

At that moment, there was a loud WHACK. Above them, her father had finally found his cutlass. He was chopping at the rope, muttering a string of guttural curses about mutineers and dragons and bait. She was too breathless to call out; if he'd known about the case on her back, certainly his greed would overcome his fear of the octopus. As Surgeon climbed, Elspeth held out hope that her father's drunken aim would keep him from cutting the rope. At that moment, Portsmouth's sword found its mark.

The limp rope dropped across her shoulders, but she didn't fall. Surgeon's talons dug into the hull. With heaving breath, he climbed. As he neared the rail, she stretched to grab it. She tried to lift herself but the weight of the case threatened to drag her back into the sea. With an animal cry of pain and rage, she tapped into a frightful strength that delivered her inch by inch toward the deck. Just as she was certain she couldn't hold on another second, she flopped over the rail and onto the deck, limp as a dead codfish.

Still clinging to the hull, Surgeon let out a yelp. Elspeth at last wiggled free of the entangling weight of the case. On trembling legs, she managed to look over the rail. The octopus had wrapped a tentacle around Surgeon's torso. Surgeon's muscles bulged in sharp relief, his scales bristling, as he kept his hold on the boards. Tentacle after tentacle slapped against the hull, rolling the ship toward the enormous cephalopod. Wooden pegs shot from their holes as boards twisted and splintered. The *Sea Dragon* in her prime might have withstood the weight of the beast, but with so much maintenance neglected under her father's command, the ship seemed fated to snap in half.

Elspeth had lost track of her father, but now he returned, brandishing a gaff pole. He leaned over the rail, trying to knock Surgeon loose. "Let go, you devil!" he screamed. "The beast wants your carcass and I aim to let him have it!"

"No!" Elspeth screamed, limping along the rail to grab her father's arm. He looked at her with confused eyes, baffled as to where she'd come from, then roughly pushed her away.

"He saved my life!" she screamed.

"He'll save us all by giving the monster something to chew on!" Her father's eyes were wild, bloodshot with inebriation.

She wasted no further words, hopping and limping toward her father's cabin. She stumbled inside, falling to the floor, thrusting her hand under the bed. Her groping fingers found the box of flares. If the octopus didn't like the touch of a single flare, it definitely wouldn't enjoy a dozen shoved down its gullet.

She hobbled her way back toward the rail. Surgeon's claws had left long gouges in the hull as the octopus dragged him ever closer toward its snapping beak. Many of the more cowardly crew members had thrown themselves into the water, swimming for the distant shore.

She pulled out a single flare and tore off the cap. It burst into white smoke and intense cherry light.

Her father screamed at her. "Those are for treasure, damn you!"

As he spoke, an enormous tentacle rose behind him.

"Move aside!" she cried.

"You worthless brat!" Spittle flew from her father's lips as he swung the gaff hook toward her.

She ducked beneath its drunken arc as she dropped the lit fuse into the box with the others. She jammed the lid shut. "You want them? Catch them!"

She threw the box as hard as she could. Her father dropped the gaff and caught the box against his chest as smoke erupted from every seam. He stumbled back against the rail as the gaff skittered across the deck and stopped at Elspeth's feet.

As the octopus had demonstrated with the shark, sometimes the only way to be rid of a monster was to feed it to another monster. She grabbed the gaff and skillfully hooked it behind her father's ankles.

His drunken eyes snapped into sudden sobriety. "Daughter?" he said, his voice suddenly calm. "What are you doing?"

"Giving the monster something to chew on," she said, pulling her father's feet out from under him so that he fell backward atop the rail. He hung in the balance, his good hand still holding the smoking box of flares to his chest as his hook hand flailed desperately to snag a rope.

Instead of a rope, the hook sank into the rubbery flesh of a tentacle. The slithering arm encircled her father's torso, pinning the box of flares against his chest. With a crunch, both box and ribcage were crushed. Her father's face went purple. The black smoke pouring from the fractured chest gave way to blinding light as the collective flares erupted in a maelstrom of hideous flame.

The ship lurched as the octopus released it. Elspeth was thrown from her feet, tumbling across the deck as the ship pitched away from the beast. She caught herself at the far rail, and found her footing a moment later as the ship groaned back toward an even keel.

She looked to where she'd last seen her father. He was gone, leaving only a faint haze of smoke where he'd tumbled over the rail. Surgeon's face was visible through this haze as his quivering limbs at last brought him to the deck. She limped to his side and gazed over. The water around the ship was black as coal.

She didn't see her father, or hear him shouting over the cries of the craven sailors who'd lost faith in the ship, all now vanishing beneath the waves as countless shark fins darted and dashed about. The storm she'd felt earlier was drawing nearer. Somehow, the mast hadn't snapped, and the mainsail still flapped in the rising wind. The storm front would carry her far from these cursed waters.

Elspeth picked up her father's fallen cutlass. She turned to gaze across the deck. The eyes of a dozen desperate seadogs sized her up carefully. She met their stares one by one, until each man blinked, or turned his face.

"Don't just stand about!" she called out. "You four! Trim those sails! You, and you! Get hammers! We'll have to make repairs on the move!" She shouted more orders, until every hand was busy, save for Surgeon.

"Don't think that saving my life means you'll get to slack off on my watch," she said, folding her arms behind her back. "Take the wheel!"

"Aye, captain," Surgeon said, loud enough for the whole crew to hear. "And where are we heading?"

"Hampton," she said, as she saw that none of the crew was going to raise an objection to Surgeon's use of her new title.

"And what of your discovery, captain?" Surgeon said, eyeing the case.

"Stow it in my cabin. We'll look it over together, if we make it through the storm in one piece."

Surgeon nodded, and dragged the case toward the captain's quarters.

With all the crew too busy to notice her, she sagged against the mast. She slid the cutlass into her rope belt. The hilt was sticky and wet. She stared at the literal blood on her hands.

It took a monster to slay a monster. The sun, the wind, and the sea, would never judge her.

The *Sea Dragon* lurched across the waves, chased by thunder, as she limped toward her new cabin. Before she went inside, she watched her crew hard at work. There was nothing like the terror of death to put a little life into them, and whip them into order. Surgeon was now at the wheel, steering the ship past the sandbars toward the relative safety of the open ocean.

Closing the door behind her, she collapsed onto her father's bed.

Her bed.

Wind swirled through the window, washing her with fresh, clean air. For a moment, at least, she was comfortable.

She stared at her ravaged hands. She closed them into fists. Gore oozed between her fingers. She closed them even tighter.

Order, safety, comfort.

The price, all along, was blood.

What was in the case?
All is revealed in **Dragonsgate: Spirits,**
Book Two of the **Dragonsgate** *trilogy!*

Books by James Maxey

Dragons

The Bitterwood Saga
Bitterwood
Dragonforge
Dragonsgate
Dawn of Dragons

The Dragon Apocalypse
Greatshadow
Hush
Witchbreaker
Cinder

The Dragonsgate Trilogy (in progress)
Dragonsgate: Devils
Dragonsgate: Spirits
Dragonsgate: Angels

Superheroes

Whoosh! Bam! Pow! Series
Nobody Gets the Girl
Burn Baby Burn
Covenant

Lightning Source UK Ltd.
Milton Keynes UK
UKHW020118020922
408190UK00006B/904